# What's That BUG?

By Nan Froman — Illustrated by Julian Mulock
Scientific Consultation by Dr. Doug Currie, Royal Ontario Museum

A Madison Press Book
produced for
Little, Brown and Company

Coleoptera

Diptera

Homo

The world is crawling with bugs. In fact, there may be as many as 30 million different kinds of insects alive today. They can be found almost everywhere — clinging to blades of grass, surviving on hot desert sands and icy mountain glaciers, burrowing deep into the soil, and scurrying through your house.

Over the centuries, scientists who study insects (called entomologists) have looked at the structures of insects' bodies to place them in large groups called orders. For instance, all insects with a pair of hard front wings that protect their fragile hind wings belong to the order *Coleoptera* — the beetles. There is an amazing variety of insects within each order — a tiny ladybug found in North America is related to the fierce-looking stag beetle of Vietnam.

The system that entomologists use to name insects was created by the Swedish naturalist Carolus Linnaeus in 1758. He placed plants and animals into groups by comparing their body parts. When he looked at insects, he grouped together those that had similar kinds of wings. The order *Diptera*, for example, consists of flying insects with one pair of wings — such as houseflies and mosquitoes. (The word "Diptera" means "two-winged" in Greek.) Later, other scientists continued to develop and refine this system.

Nine of the most familiar orders of insects are included here (there are twenty-eight altogether). They are presented in the sequence that many scientists think they first appeared on earth. From the well-known backyard bug to its less familiar exotic cousin, looking at insects the way entomologists do can help us to understand some of the most fascinating creatures in the world.

said the man who ordered the insects

On a sunny summer day, flashes of color dance and dart over the surface of a lake. These are dragonflies and damselflies and they belong to the order *Odonata*, one of the most ancient groups of insects in the world. Scientists have discovered 300-million-year-old fossils of giant dragonflies (below) whose wings stretched 30 inches (76 cm) from tip to tip — as far across as a seagull's. Even today, they can boast wingspans of up to seven inches (18 cm).

Dragonflies and damselflies have sharp mouthparts that are designed for chewing ("Odonata" comes from the Greek words for "teeth on jaws"). Their four slender wings can propel them swiftly through the air, and their huge compound eyes (made up of nearly 30,000 lenses) let them see in almost every direction at once. No wonder they can catch mosquitoes, flies, bees, and butterflies on the wing! Very large dragonflies sometimes even prey on hummingbirds.

## Eastern Blue Darner

Darners are among the largest, fastest, and most powerful dragonflies. At nearly five inches (13 cm) long, they can speed through the air at 35 miles (56 km) per hour. They are ferocious hunters who capture their prey in midair, snapping their long legs shut around their victims. Darners hunt mosquitoes and small moths, but they can also capture bees, butterflies, and even other dragonflies.

## Broad-winged Damselfly

How can you tell a damselfly from a dragonfly? They may look alike at first, but damselflies are usually smaller and thinner than dragonflies. And their heads are oval-shaped rather than round. Damselflies cannot fly as fast as dragonflies, and when they land, they fold their delicate wings together. Their larger cousins always keep their wings spread out horizontally.

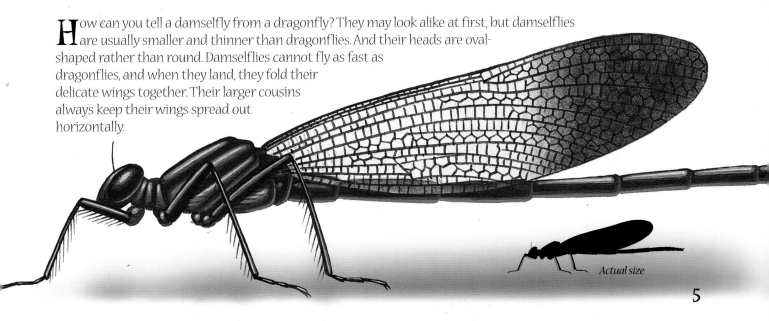

*Actual size*

The order *Orthoptera* contains nature's musicians and high jumpers — crickets, grasshoppers, and katydids — but it also includes mantids, walkingsticks, and cockroaches. Until recently, scientists had grouped all of these insects together because their bodies are similar in some ways. Those that fly have straight wings ("Orthoptera" means "straight wings" in Greek), and they all have jaws designed for chewing. But as experts learn more, they are starting to think that cockroaches, mantids, and walkingsticks should be grouped separately from Orthoptera. After all, none of them can jump or make music!

## Katydid

Disguised as a leaf, the katydid rests in trees during the day and waits until sundown to become active. On summer evenings, you might hear a group of them singing together. If their song is answered by another group, the music sometimes sounds like the words "katy did, katy didn't."

*Actual size*

## Praying Mantis

Blending in almost perfectly with its surroundings, this Vietnamese praying mantis lies in wait for its next meal. The mantis will stay very still until a butterfly, moth, fly, bee, or grasshopper comes within reach. Then it strikes quickly, seizing the insect with its spiky front legs. Some of the larger species of praying mantis can grow to be seven inches (18 cm) in length. These giants hunt frogs, lizards, and hummingbirds. Mantids are the only insects that can swivel their heads around to look in every direction.

## How do grasshoppers and crickets sing?

Grasshoppers and crickets "sing" by rubbing one body part against another. Crickets and long-horned grasshoppers rub the sharp edge of one front wing along a ridge on the other. The sound made by a single stroke of the front wings is called a pulse. The hotter it is outside, the faster the pulse rate.

6

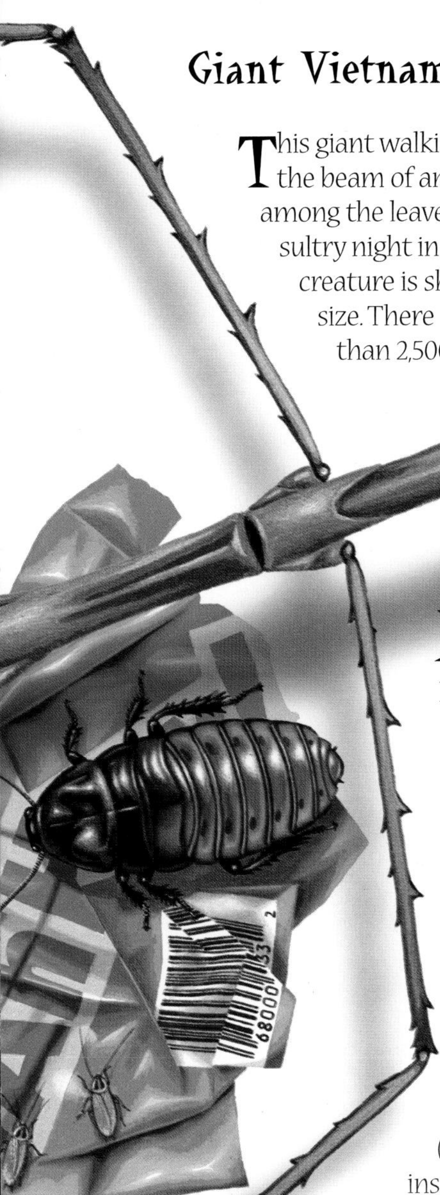

## Giant Vietnamese Walkingstick

This giant walkingstick (below) appeared in the beam of an entomologist's flashlight among the leaves of a catalpa tree one sultry night in Vietnam. The amazing creature is shown here at life size. There are more than 2,500 species of walkingstick, living mainly in tropical climates. Only 29 species can be found in North America, and they are usually only two or three inches (5–8 cm) long.

All walkingsticks are harmless, leaf-eating creatures. To protect themselves from predators, they will either hide by lying very still along the side of a twig or drop to the ground and fold their legs close to their bodies so that they look like sticks.

## Hissing Cockroach and Domestic Cockroach

No one likes to find a cockroach in the kitchen. These insects (left) can be serious pests, feeding on anything they can find, even garbage. Although they have two pairs of wings, they are fast runners and prefer to use their legs to escape danger. Occasionally a tropical species like the huge hissing cockroach (seen at upper left) creeps into a shipment of fruit and makes its way to northern climates. Found in Madagascar, off the coast of Africa, this cockroach can force air through small breathing holes in its abdomen and make a hissing sound to scare off predators such as birds and lizards.

## North American Cricket and Vietnamese Cricket

A ⅝-inch (1.5 cm) long North American house cricket (below left) wouldn't stand a chance against one of its tropical cousins! House crickets live indoors almost all over the world. You can hear their chirping both day and night, but they usually come out after dark to find crumbs of leftover food. The 1 ¾-inch (4.5 cm) long cricket from Vietnam (below right) is a carnivore that devours other insects for nourishment.

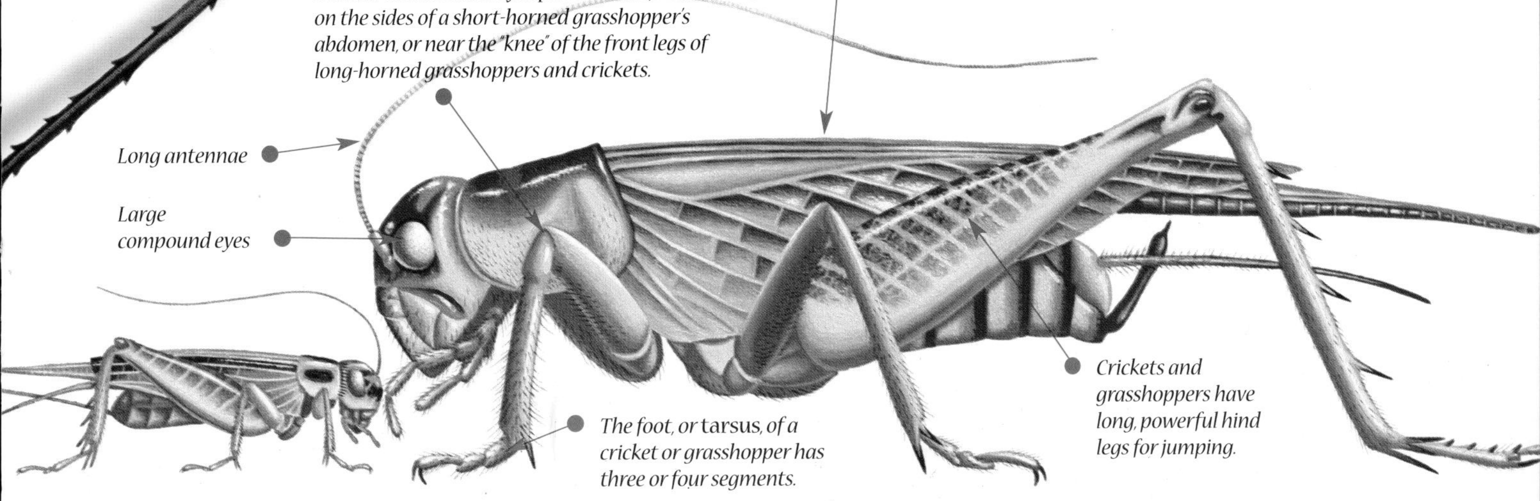

*The front pair of wings is long and leathery and is not used for flying. The hind wings can be folded underneath this pair.*

*Oval eardrums called tympana can be found on the sides of a short-horned grasshopper's abdomen, or near the "knee" of the front legs of long-horned grasshoppers and crickets.*

*Long antennae*

*Large compound eyes*

*The foot, or tarsus, of a cricket or grasshopper has three or four segments.*

*Crickets and grasshoppers have long, powerful hind legs for jumping.*

7

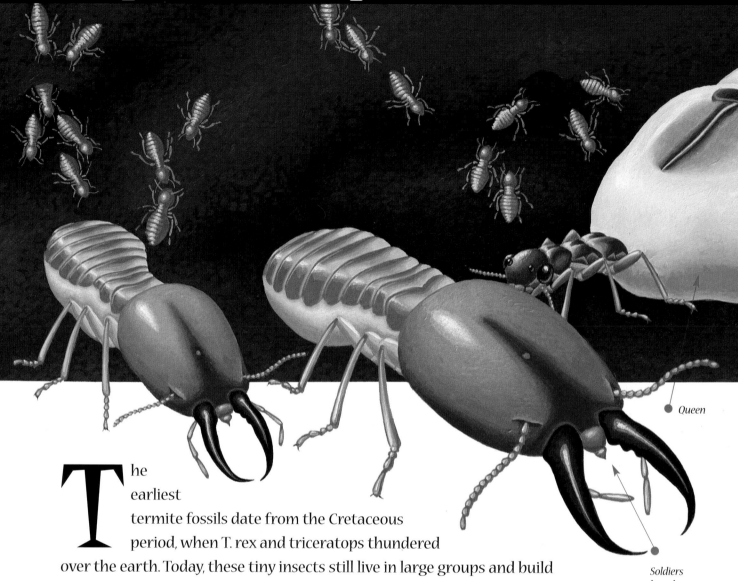

Queen

Soldiers have large, dark heads and powerful jaws.

**T**he earliest termite fossils date from the Cretaceous period, when T. rex and triceratops thundered over the earth. Today, these tiny insects still live in large groups and build elaborate nests. Termites that live in North America and Mexico hide their nests underground or drill them into wood. But in Africa and Australia, termite mounds sometimes tower 30 feet (9 meters) above the ground like giant mushrooms.

## Termite Pests

Termites move from one part of a piece of wood to another through mud tunnels they construct.

**N**orth American and Mexican termites live in underground nests, but they can dig mud tunnels from their nests to the wooden parts of houses. Since they need a humid environment to survive, they build walls of mud around a section of the wood, sealing themselves inside while they feed. When experts spot these mud tunnels and walls, along with plaster-like droppings, they suspect a harmful termite infestation.

Soldier   Worker

These worker termites are safely sealed inside their feeding area.

Actual size

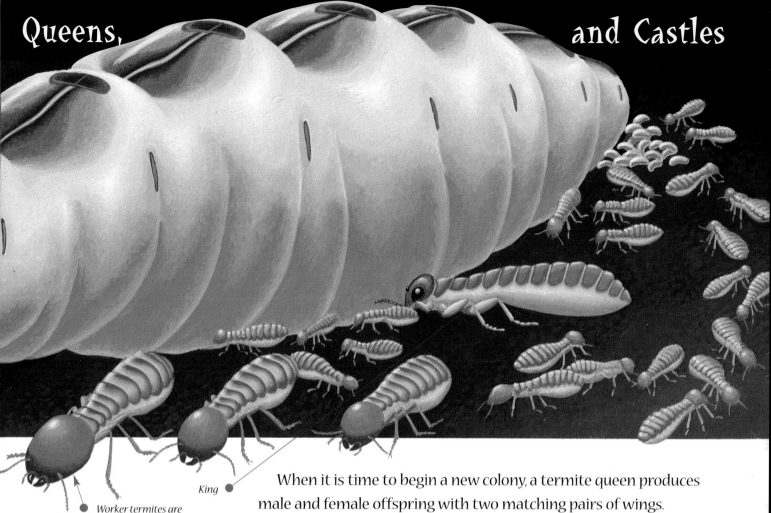

*King*

*Worker termites are blind and have soft bodies.*

When it is time to begin a new colony, a termite queen produces male and female offspring with two matching pairs of wings. ("Isoptera" means "equal wings" in Greek.) These winged termites swarm from the nest, find a partner, shed their silvery wings, and dig a nest in the soil. A pair seal themselves inside a royal chamber and become the king and queen of a new colony (above). After the queen starts producing eggs (she may lay many thousands every day), her abdomen swells so much that she resembles a large, glistening sausage. At first the king and queen feed their young and tend to the nest, but blind worker termites soon take over these tasks. They keep the nest in good repair, find food, and feed and groom the other termites. Soldier termites are also blind, but they can use their long, powerful jaws to attack predators such as ants.

## Mud Castles

The most amazing termites of all build castle-like mounds on the grassy plains of Africa. These mounds can house families of a million or more insects. The outer walls are made up of soil mixed with termite saliva. The inner walls consist of droppings combined with wood fragments. Within the mound is a royal chamber for the queen and king, a nursery for young termites, and fungus gardens where the termites grow mushrooms. The mushrooms contain an enzyme that helps the termites digest the tough fibers in the plants they eat.

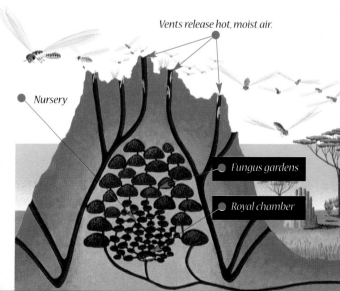

*Vents release hot, moist air.*

*Nursery*

*Fungus gardens*

*Royal chamber*

True bugs belong to the order *Hemiptera* and there are a lot of them — 50,000 species live all over the world. This order includes green stink bugs and their brightly colored tropical cousins. These bugs have scent glands that can release a nauseating smell when the insects are threatened. Hemiptera also includes water striders that seem to skate across ponds and lakes, giant water bugs fierce enough to attack small fish or frogs, and assassin and ambush bugs — as crafty as their names suggest.

How can you tell if a bug is a true bug? All true bugs have two sets of wings. The front pair is leathery at the base and transparent at the tip ("Hemiptera" means "half wings" in Greek). Between the wings you will often find a beautiful triangular shield. True bugs also have mouthparts that look like very fine, sharp beaks. Some of them feed on plant juices, others on the body fluids of insects or other small animals. A few true bugs will even suck the blood of humans!

Actual size

## Shield-backed Bug

The shiny colors and bright patterns on these tropical shield-backed bugs (left and above) may serve as a warning to predators that they taste bad. Shield-backed bugs defend themselves by releasing a smelly liquid from scent glands underneath their bodies.

## Green Stink Bug

Like its tropical kin, the jewel-like North American stink bug (opposite) can also emit a foul-smelling fluid when threatened. This bug can be found feeding on plant juices in gardens or orchards. It has a sharp beak that it uses for piercing the surface of a plant and sucking up sap. While most stink bugs feed on plants, a few dine on caterpillars and beetle larvae, sucking up their insides.

# Hemiptera — Cunning and Deadly

## Tropical Assassin Bug

Their unusual shapes and colors help tropical assassin bugs (above and below) blend in perfectly with flowers and leaves. There, they lie in wait until a flying insect comes within reach. Then the assassin bug grabs its victim and paralyzes it by injecting poisonous saliva through its needle-sharp beak.

Some assassins suck blood from mammals, birds, or reptiles. A few, found in Texas, Central America, and South America, will even bite people, transmitting a serious illness called Chagas' disease.

*Actual size*

## Masked Assassin Bug

The young North American assassin bug (above) is sometimes called a "dust bug." That's because it disguises its sticky body with dust and lint as it hunts for insect prey inside houses. A young assassin bug is similar to a fully grown bug (below), except that it has no wings.

The adult assassin bug also hunts other insects, sneaking up on them until it is close enough to attack with its dagger-like beak. It surprises its victims with a painful bite, grabs them with its powerful front legs, then sucks out their body fluids.

The hairy front legs of some assassins are covered with a thick, sticky liquid that attracts other insects, who are quickly trapped and eaten.

## Giant Water Bug

The giant water bug is among the largest of all insects — sometimes up to three inches (8 cm) long — big enough to grapple with snakes, frogs, and fish. This bug captures prey with its front legs, then uses its sharp beak to inject enough poison to rapidly kill its victim. It then slowly sucks out the nourishing internal juices. With oar-like back legs and special breathing tubes placed underneath its abdomen, the giant water bug is well adapted to life in ponds and streams across North America. In Asia, the giant water bug is considered a delicacy.

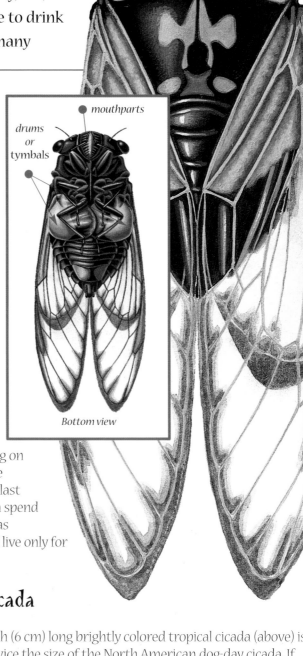

**B**uzzing cicadas, weirdly shaped treehoppers, tiny aphids and leafhoppers, spittlebugs hiding inside a mass of bubbles, annoying whiteflies — all of these unusual creatures belong to the large order of insects known as *Homoptera*.

Homoptera are closely related to true bugs. They, too, have sucking, beak-like mouthparts, which they use to drink the sap from trees and plants. And like true bugs, many

## Dog-day Cicada

*The full-grown dog-day cicada*

**I**f you have ever heard a loud buzzing sound on a hot summer afternoon, then you have probably heard the male cicada. These large insects have special sound-producing organs below their abdomens.

The female dog-day cicada — named for the hot "dog days" of summer — lays her eggs on a twig. After an egg hatches, the young larva, or nymph, drops to the ground and burrows into the soil, where it feeds on roots. Several years later, it climbs up the plant it has been feeding on and crawls out of its hard protective covering, a full-grown cicada at last (left). Some species of cicada spend as long as seventeen years as underground nymphs and live only for a month as adults!

*Transparent wings — the front pair is much longer than the hind pair.*

*Nymph's outer covering*

*drums or tymbals*

*mouthparts*

*Bottom view*

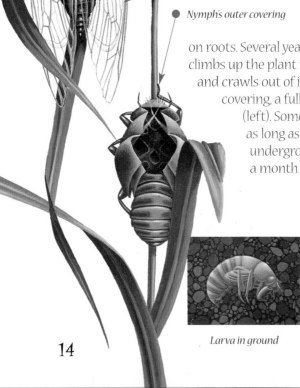

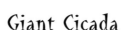

*Larva in ground*

## Giant Cicada

**T**he 2½-inch (6 cm) long brightly colored tropical cicada (above) is almost twice the size of the North American dog-day cicada. If you look closely at the bottom view of this insect, you will see its sharp mouthparts — designed for piercing plants — as well as the two large round *tymbals*, or "drums," that it uses to make its sound. These huge cicadas can be extremely noisy.

Homoptera have four wings, though theirs are completely transparent. ("Homoptera" means "similar wings" in Greek.)

A large number of the insects in this group can also be serious pests to trees and plants. Some leafhoppers suck so much sap from plants that they destroy the green pigment called chlorophyll that the plants need to make food. Aphids can pass on diseases to peaches, corn, and beans. And by pressing their eggs into small slits in twigs, cicadas — as well as tree- and leafhoppers — can stunt the growth of trees.

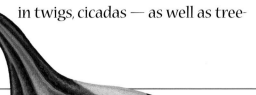

North America

## Treehoppers

**S**ome of these small jumping insects look like knights' helmets. Others could easily be mistaken for a thorn. Treehoppers come in such unusual shapes because the upper part of the thorax — the body section closest to their heads — is so large. Many treehoppers, especially the tropical ones, also display bright colors and beautiful patterns.

If a wasp hovers over young Central or South American treehoppers resting together on a plant stem, they will produce a vibration in their bodies that travels along the stem to their mother. She hurries to defend her babies, sending the wasp on its way with a powerful kick from her hind legs.

North America

Trinidad

Actual size

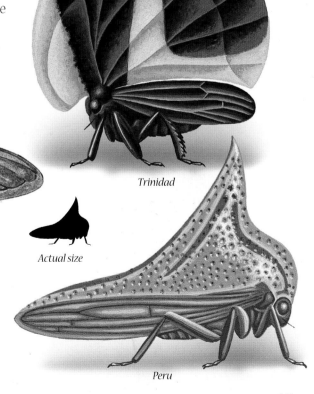

Ecuador

Peru

There are 350,000 species of beetle and they can be found crawling, burrowing, flying, and swimming on every continent except Antarctica. Beetles live everywhere but in the ocean. And each species has adapted to suit its environment. A beetle found in the Namibian desert can raise its body on stilt-like legs to protect itself from the burning sand! Amazingly, entomologists believe there are still millions of kinds of beetles yet to be discovered in the world's rain forests.

*Coleoptera* range from huge tropical species, like the African Goliath beetle, which is almost as big as a man's hand, to familiar garden dwellers, like the tiny ladybug. Almost all beetles have tough front wings called *elytra*. The elytra are often colorful and carry beautiful patterns. But they also act like a suit of armor, protecting the beetle's transparent hind wings, which are used for flying. ("Coleoptera" means "sheath wings" in Greek.) Beetles have mouthparts designed for chewing all kinds of foods — from other insects to tree bark, animal dung, and even cloth. Burying beetles will even feed on dead mice and shrews. A male and female will bury a dead mouse and make it into their nest, then feed on the mouse and regurgitate it to nourish their young.

## Ladybird Beetles

The most familiar ladybird beetles (often called "ladybugs") are red with black spots, but they can also be black, yellow, or orange, with between two and twenty-four spots (above). Their bright colors are a signal to birds and other insects that they are poisonous. When danger threatens, a ladybird beetle may lie on its back and pretend to be dead, or squirt a foul-smelling yellow liquid from between its leg joints.

Ladybird beetles are helpful to humans because they eat garden pests, like aphids. These little beetles were considered special during the Middle Ages because they ate the insects that were destroying grapevines. And in 1887, they were brought to California from Australia to help control other insects that were attacking citrus groves.

## Click Beetle

The click beetle (left and below) is the gymnast of the insect world. When it is lying on its back, it can make a "clicking" sound as it flips itself over, landing neatly on its feet. A flexible joint between its thorax and its abdomen makes this stunt possible. Most click beetles eat plants, and some tropical species glow at night.

*Actual size*

## Firefly or Lightning Bug

The twinkling yellow, orange, or green lights of fireflies make summer evenings magical. Male fireflies (left) have light-producing organs on their abdomens that they flash to attract mates. Wingless females and their young both give off light and are called glowworms.

Each species of firefly has its own light-flashing pattern. The females of some predatory species can imitate the flashing of another species, allowing them to attract male fireflies and then eat them. In tropical Asia, many fireflies — both male and female — will rest in a tree while the males flash their lights in sync, creating "firefly trees."

## Metallic Wood-boring Beetle

The metallic wood-boring beetle (right) is also called a jewel beetle because of its shiny coloring and elegant shape. Although they are difficult to catch because they are such fast runners and fliers, they are a favorite among insect collectors. The larvae of these beetles often make their homes in dead trees and logs.

## Why are beetles so successful?

Beetles survive so well on our planet for two reasons: they have tough, compact bodies that allow them to hide, find food, and lay eggs in places other insects could never go, and they can feed on almost every kind of plant. Beetles make use of every plant part — from underground roots and seeds to bark, leaves, flowers, and fruit. Some beetles even chew around the stems of poisonous plants to let the deadly sap drain away before they begin their meal.

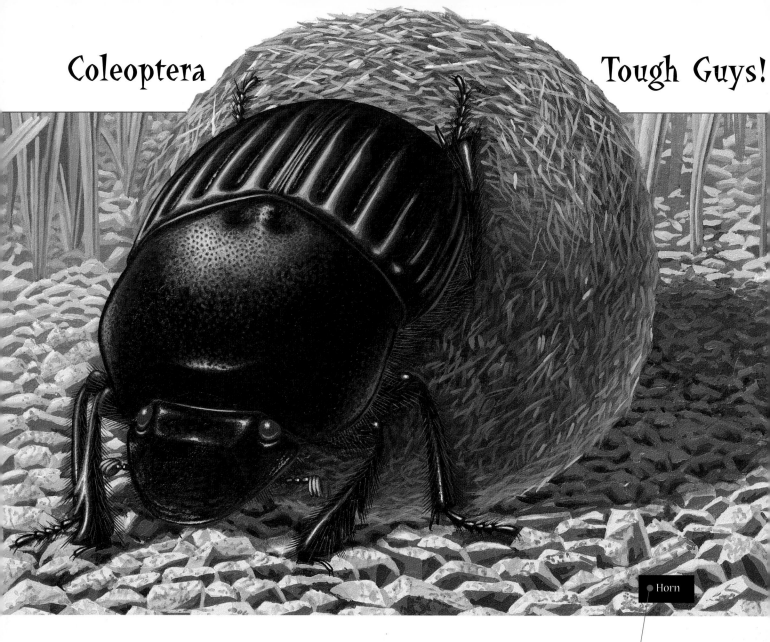

Horn

Antenna

## Dung-rolling Scarab Beetle

Tropical dung-rolling scarab beetles (above) will chew off a piece of animal dung, shape it into a ball, and roll it along the ground. Working in pairs, one beetle will pull the ball of dung while its mate pushes with its hind legs. The busy scarabs then bury the dung ball in the soil and the female lays her eggs, either on top of it or nearby. That way, when the young hatch, they not only have a ready food supply, but they are protected as well. The ancient Egyptians depicted their sun god, Ra, as a scarab beetle rolling the sun, like a dung ball, across the sky.

## Bombardier Beetle

The North American bombardier beetle (left) has a powerful means of defense. Its body contains glands that produce a poisonous liquid, which the beetle can spray out with a loud "pop." The hot fluid evaporates into what looks like a puff of smoke that can burn and blind such predators as ants, spiders, mice, frogs, or birds. The beetle will fire over and over again until its enemy backs off.

18

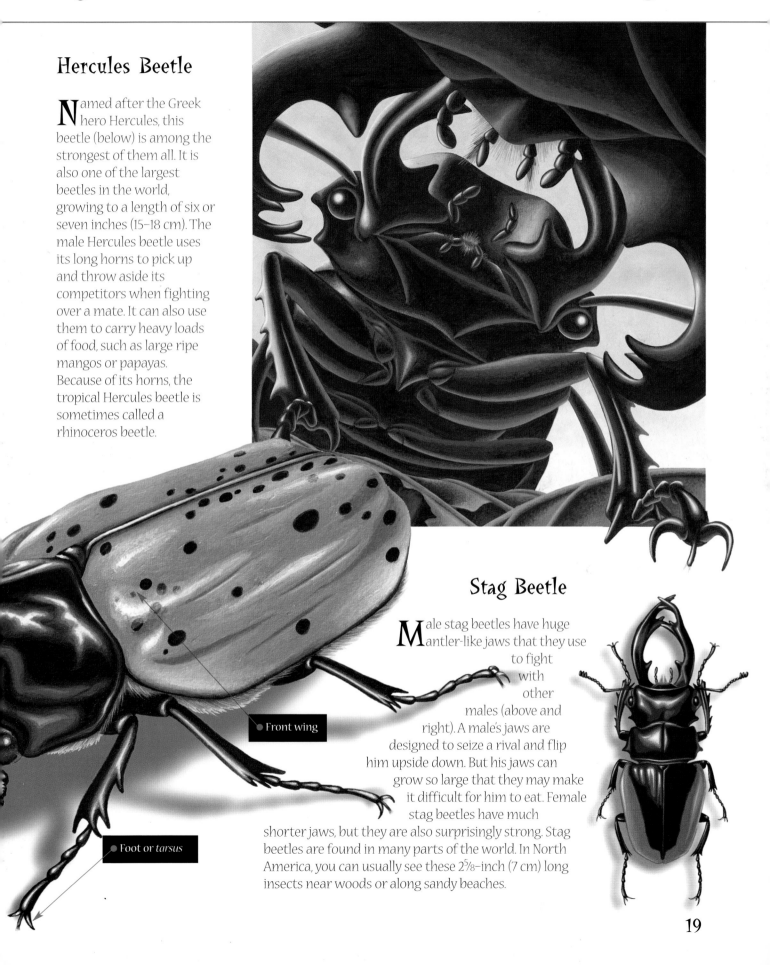

# Dung Rollers, Stink Bombers, Bullies, and Fighters...

## Hercules Beetle

Named after the Greek hero Hercules, this beetle (below) is among the strongest of them all. It is also one of the largest beetles in the world, growing to a length of six or seven inches (15–18 cm). The male Hercules beetle uses its long horns to pick up and throw aside its competitors when fighting over a mate. It can also use them to carry heavy loads of food, such as large ripe mangos or papayas. Because of its horns, the tropical Hercules beetle is sometimes called a rhinoceros beetle.

Front wing

Foot or *tarsus*

## Stag Beetle

Male stag beetles have huge antler-like jaws that they use to fight with other males (above and right). A male's jaws are designed to seize a rival and flip him upside down. But his jaws can grow so large that they may make it difficult for him to eat. Female stag beetles have much shorter jaws, but they are also surprisingly strong. Stag beetles are found in many parts of the world. In North America, you can usually see these 2⅝-inch (7 cm) long insects near woods or along sandy beaches.

**F**rom a pretty skipper fluttering above a field of wildflowers to the stunning tropical blue morpho, *Lepidoptera* includes some of the most beautiful and fascinating of all insects. Even as caterpillars, butterflies and moths can be amazing. Some have sharp spines to protect them from predators, while others sport bright colors that warn, "Poison. Do not eat me." Gypsy moth caterpillars can strip huge trees of their leaves, and silkworms can spin silk for fine scarves and ties.

The name "Lepidoptera" comes from the Greek words *lepido*, meaning "scale", and *ptera*, which means "wings." Butterflies and moths have what look like scales on all four of their wings, and these will brush off like dust if you touch them. The scales are actually tiny, flat hairs that also cover the insects' bodies and legs. They create the colors and patterns we see on butterflies and moths.

*Actual size*

*Actual size*

## Blue Morpho

**T**his tropical butterfly is famous for its spectacular wings, which shimmer in shades from brilliant sky blue to deep purple (top and left). The scales on the blue morpho's wings have tiny ridges that create shiny colors when light strikes them. A resting blue morpho (right) is well disguised — the dull colors on the underside of its wings blend in perfectly with dry leaves or tree bark.

## Monarch

This butterfly (below) may look delicate, but it is famous for making long migrations. Every fall, monarchs throughout North America fly south to the milder climates of California, Florida, Cuba, and Mexico. The longest of these flights is nearly 2,000 miles (3,200 km)! These same butterflies, or their offspring, head back north the next spring.

Monarchs are rarely attacked by birds or insects. This is because their caterpillars feed on the milkweed plant, which contains a poison that becomes concentrated in the wings of adult butterflies. If a bird eats a monarch, it becomes very sick and from then on will avoid monarchs — or any other butterfly that looks like one.

*Actual size*

## Mourning Cloak

The mourning cloak is one of the first butterflies you are likely to see in the spring. As soon as a spiny caterpillar hatches from its egg, it feasts on willow, elm, and poplar leaves. As it grows, the caterpillar sheds its skin and, when the time is right, finds a safe spot to form a chrysalis, or cocoon. After ten to fifteen days, the chrysalis splits open and a butterfly emerges.

With a lifespan of nearly a year, the mourning cloak is one of the longest-living North American butterflies. Some mourning cloaks migrate to warmer climates when winter approaches, but others remain where they are, taking shelter in unheated buildings or under loose tree bark. These butterflies freeze solid over the winter, but in the spring they thaw out and fly again.

*Actual size*

## Viceroy

Although the North American viceroy (left) is not poisonous, it looks so much like the monarch butterfly that it is fairly safe from predators. The differences are subtle, but you can see them: viceroys are smaller than monarchs, they have a narrow black line that curves across their hind wings, and a single row of white spots around the edges of their wings. Even the caterpillars of the viceroy are unlikely to be eaten — their shape and color make them look like bird droppings!

# Lepidoptera — Colorful Daytrippers and

How can you tell if an insect is a butterfly or a moth? These bug beauties may appear similar, but there are many differences between them. Butterflies are usually seen flying during the daylight hours. When they land, they hold their wings close together. Most moths, on the other hand, are night fliers, and when they are not flying they keep their

*Actual size*

## The Magnificent Paradise Birdwing

Predators avoid this large, brightly colored tropical butterfly (above). But its extraordinary beauty puts it at risk because so many people want to collect it. This butterfly and other members of the birdwing family are the only insects in the world that are protected by an international agreement that controls the trading of species threatened with extinction.

*Actual size*

## Swallowtail

Though this specimen was found in Europe, you can see swallowtails (left) sipping nectar from flowers all over the world. These strikingly colored butterflies belong to a large group of butterflies that includes the birdwings of southeast Asia and Australia. The caterpillar of the swallowtail is known as the "skunk" of the butterfly world because it gives off a nasty smell when it is disturbed.

## Luna Moth

Named after the ancient Roman goddess of the moon, the Luna (below) is the largest moth found in North America. This beautiful ghostly flier emerges from a cocoon that a spiny green caterpillar makes in a leaf on the ground. Like many large moths, the adult Luna doesn't eat at all. So many Luna moths are killed by pesticides and pollution that it has become a rare species.

*Actual size*

## Sunset Moth

This stunning tropical moth (opposite page) flies during the day, its iridescent colors shining in the sun. Its scientific name, *Urania ripheus*, means "family of the heavenly ones."

# Creatures that Fly by Night

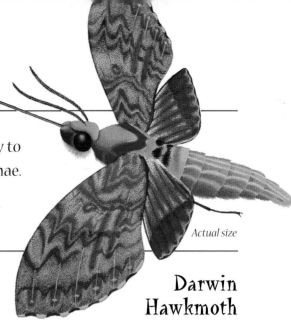

*Actual size*

**Darwin Hawkmoth**

wings spread out or curled around their bodies. Another way to tell moths and butterflies apart is by looking at their antennae. Moths have feathery or straight ones, while butterflies have antennae with little knobs on the ends.

The Darwin hawkmoth's one-foot (30 cm) long proboscis lets it drink from long-necked flowers that are impossible for many other insects to feed upon (above). It is most often seen at dawn and dusk, hovering around tropical blossoms like a hummingbird.

*Sunset Moth*
*Top view*
*Actual size*

*Sunset Moth*
*Bottom view*
*Actual size*

## Pollution and the Peppered Moth

In the 1800s, factory smokestacks spread coal dust over the trunks of trees in England. As a result, a particular kind of moth that often landed on tree trunks became darker in color. The darker color meant these moths were better camouflaged against the soot-covered trees, giving them a greater chance of escaping predators. Since coal is not used as much as it once was, these moths are now returning to their original color, which blends in perfectly with lichen-covered bark.

The pesky members of the *Diptera* family have been buzzing around since Jurassic times. The common housefly is the most familiar member of this order, but it has a number of vicious cousins like the huge tropical robber fly. This fly dives onto the backs of other insects, sticks its beak into their necks, and injects them with a poison that kills them and dissolves their insides — which the robber fly then sips up like a milkshake. Other Diptera include fruit flies and such bloodsuckers as mosquitoes, blackflies, tsetse flies, and horseflies.

But flies are not all bad. They prey on other insect pests and are themselves a source of

# The Housefly

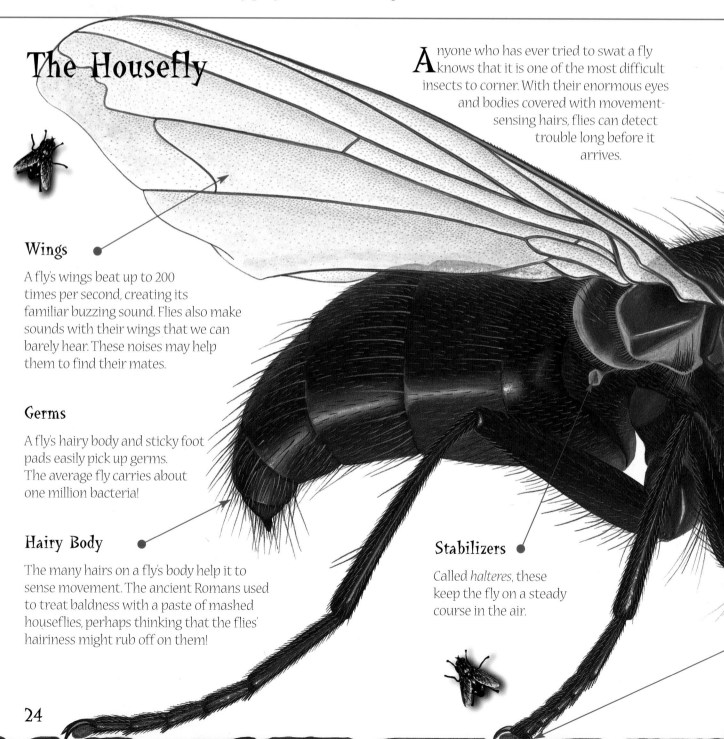

Anyone who has ever tried to swat a fly knows that it is one of the most difficult insects to corner. With their enormous eyes and bodies covered with movement-sensing hairs, flies can detect trouble long before it arrives.

## Wings

A fly's wings beat up to 200 times per second, creating its familiar buzzing sound. Flies also make sounds with their wings that we can barely hear. These noises may help them to find their mates.

## Germs

A fly's hairy body and sticky foot pads easily pick up germs. The average fly carries about one million bacteria!

## Hairy Body

The many hairs on a fly's body help it to sense movement. The ancient Romans used to treat baldness with a paste of mashed houseflies, perhaps thinking that the flies' hairiness might rub off on them!

## Stabilizers

Called *halteres*, these keep the fly on a steady course in the air.

food for dragonflies, mantids, and many other animals. Many flies, such as the nectar-drinking hover fly, even help to pollinate flowers. The only way a fly can avoid being eaten — or swatted with a newspaper — is to take flight.

While most flying insects have four wings, Diptera have two. The name Diptera actually means "two-winged" in Greek. Little drumstick-shaped organs under each wing help keep flies steady in the air. These organs, called *halteres*, also enable Diptera to perform dazzling loop-the-loops and other aerial feats.

## Compound Eyes

Flies have two large compound eyes. Instead of having one lens as we do, each of their eyes is made up of 4,000 six-sided lenses pointing in different directions. Each lens sees a small part of an image. If a fly looks at a flower, it sees it in many pieces, like a mosaic pattern. Flies see colors, and some experiments suggest that red is their favorite color. The eyes of male flies are larger than those of females, possibly to help them find mates and spot their rivals more easily.

### Stalk-Eyed Fly

This fly has been called the "hammerhead shark" of the insect world because of the eye stalks on either side of its head. Having its eyes stick out so far may help this insect hunt for food. Males also use their eye stalks to battle with rivals over mates. Most species of the stalk-eyed fly are tropical. Only one species is found in North America, often on skunk cabbage plants.

## When a housefly is hungry...

A fly uses its antennae to detect smells and find food. Flies are attracted to sweet smells as well as to strong, unpleasant ones. When a fly lands on a peach, for example, it probes the fruit with taste receptors in its feet, then unfolds a nose-like tube called a proboscis to test the food again. If the peach passes this second taste test, the fly spits saliva onto the fruit to soften it. (Flies cannot suck up solid food.) Finally it uses a tiny spongy cushion at the end of its proboscis to suck up the sweet liquid.

### Sticky Feet

A fly's sticky foot pads help it to climb slippery surfaces, such as windows, or crawl upside down on ceilings.

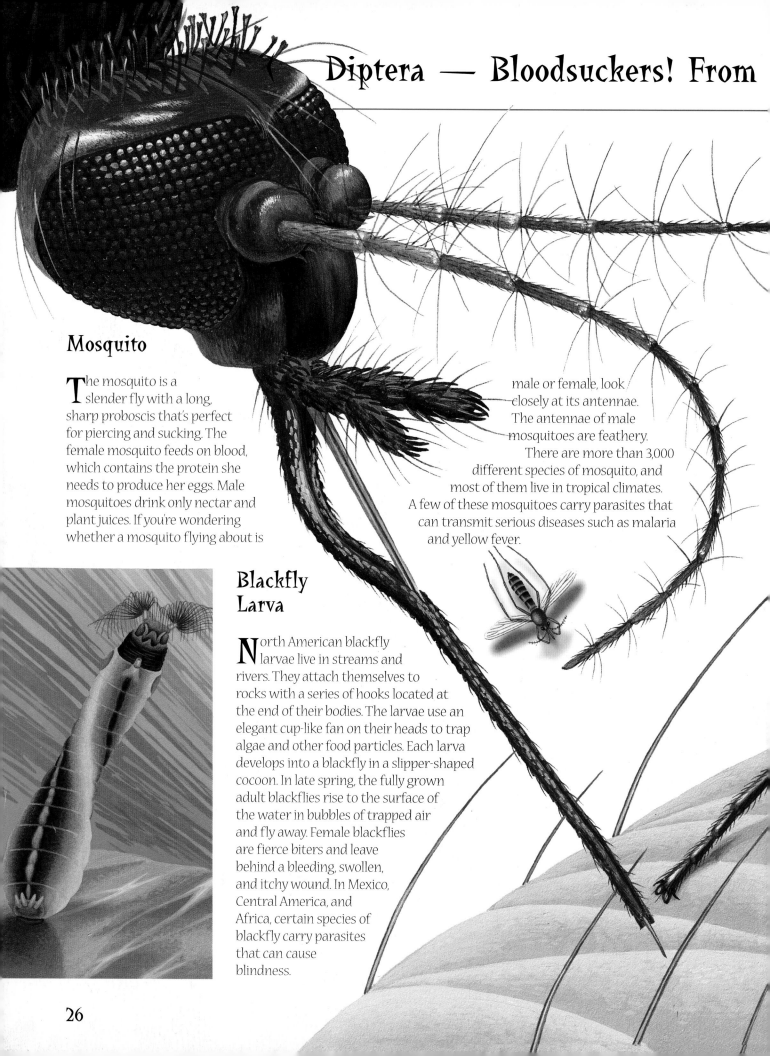

## Mosquito

The mosquito is a slender fly with a long, sharp proboscis that's perfect for piercing and sucking. The female mosquito feeds on blood, which contains the protein she needs to produce her eggs. Male mosquitoes drink only nectar and plant juices. If you're wondering whether a mosquito flying about is male or female, look closely at its antennae. The antennae of male mosquitoes are feathery. There are more than 3,000 different species of mosquito, and most of them live in tropical climates. A few of these mosquitoes carry parasites that can transmit serious diseases such as malaria and yellow fever.

## Blackfly Larva

North American blackfly larvae live in streams and rivers. They attach themselves to rocks with a series of hooks located at the end of their bodies. The larvae use an elegant cup-like fan on their heads to trap algae and other food particles. Each larva develops into a blackfly in a slipper-shaped cocoon. In late spring, the fully grown adult blackflies rise to the surface of the water in bubbles of trapped air and fly away. Female blackflies are fierce biters and leave behind a bleeding, swollen, and itchy wound. In Mexico, Central America, and Africa, certain species of blackfly carry parasites that can cause blindness.

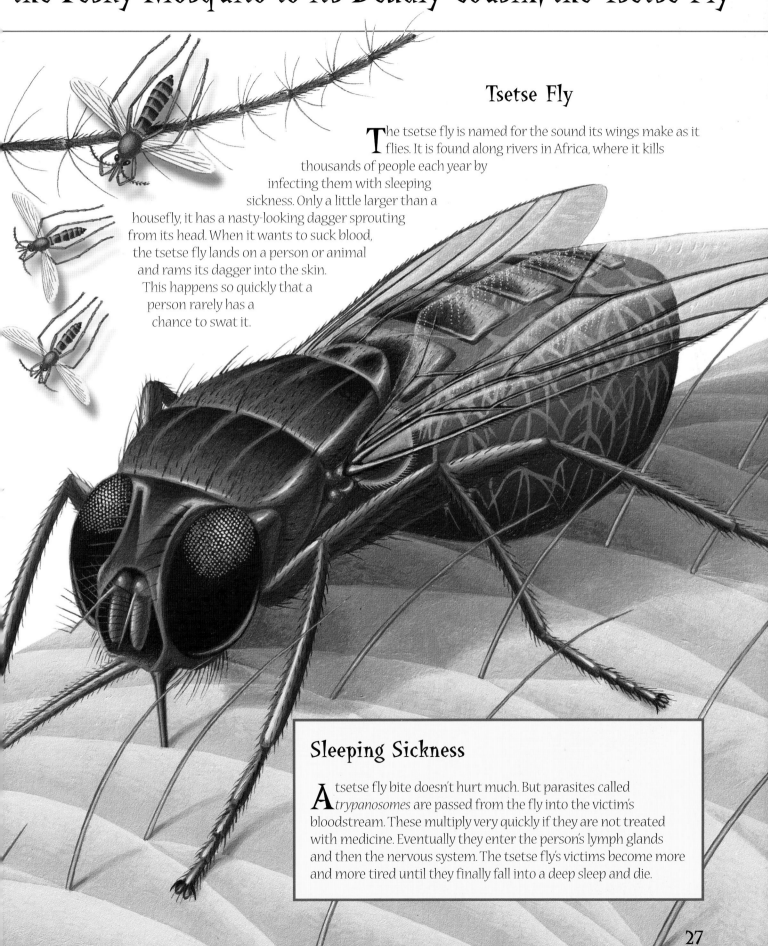

# the Pesky Mosquito to its Deadly Cousin, the Tsetse Fly

## Tsetse Fly

The tsetse fly is named for the sound its wings make as it flies. It is found along rivers in Africa, where it kills thousands of people each year by infecting them with sleeping sickness. Only a little larger than a housefly, it has a nasty-looking dagger sprouting from its head. When it wants to suck blood, the tsetse fly lands on a person or animal and rams its dagger into the skin. This happens so quickly that a person rarely has a chance to swat it.

## Sleeping Sickness

A tsetse fly bite doesn't hurt much. But parasites called *trypanosomes* are passed from the fly into the victim's bloodstream. These multiply very quickly if they are not treated with medicine. Eventually they enter the person's lymph glands and then the nervous system. The tsetse fly's victims become more and more tired until they finally fall into a deep sleep and die.

# Hymenoptera (Hy•me•'nop•te•ra)

**W**hy do bees, ants, and wasps belong to the same group of insects? Most *Hymenoptera* have four transparent wings. ("Hymenoptera" means "membrane wings" in Greek.) Their smaller hind wings are attached to a larger front pair by tiny hooks. Bees, wasps, and ants also all have narrow "waists" which allow them to move the back ends of their bodies freely to lay eggs or to sting.

Bees are among the champion fliers of the insect world. You will most often see them hovering around flowers, drinking nectar and collecting pollen. Most bees live by themselves, building their nests in tree hollows or under the soil. But honey bees and bumblebees live in colonies made up of a queen, female workers, and males called "drones."

Wasps feed on nectar and sweet sap from trees. Like bees, most wasps live by themselves, laying their eggs in underground tunnels lined with mud, in hollow logs, or on leaves. But some, such as yellow jacket wasps (the kind that ruin a picnic), live in groups of up to 5,000.

## Honey Bee

**A** honey bee gathers nectar from flowers and collects it in a special sac in its neck. It is then turned into honey. Back in the nest, the bee spits the liquid honey out into a honeycomb cell, where it provides food for the hive's larvae as well as nourishment for the winter.

A honey bee is quick to sting to defend its colony. After it stings, it leaves a barbed spear in your flesh. This stinger is actually part of the bee's abdomen. Without it, the bee dies — having given up its life to save the colony.

## Dancing Bees

**W**hen honey bees want to announce that they have found a good source of nectar and pollen, they spread the news with a special dance. If the flowers are nearby, a honey bee will fly back to her hive and "dance" in a small circle on a comb, first in one direction and then in the other. When the other bees see what she is doing, they will join in. Then they all fly out of the hive, following the flower scent on the leader to find the food.

If the flowers are far away, the leader will walk in a figure-eight pattern inside the hive, waggling her abdomen as she moves along the middle part in a straight line (left). Depending on how fast or slow the leader walks and on how much she waggles, the bees will know how far away the food is. The dance also tells the other bees the exact direction they should fly.

**Bald-faced Hornet**

In the spring, a female bald-faced hornet will chew bits of wood into pulp. She spits out the wads of pulp, and then smooths them out to make layers of six-sided cells for her eggs. Finally, she wraps the entire nest in a papery cover, leaving an entrance hole at the bottom. Now the female hornet can lay her eggs. Once the eggs hatch, the mother hornet feeds her larvae partly chewed insects. After several weeks, the young develop into adult hornets.

Bald-faced wasps protect their nests, and they will sting if they are disturbed. Their stinger consists of a tube attached to a sac of venom. Unlike bees, hornets and wasps can sting more than once by pulling out their stingers and using them again.

# Tarantula Hawk Wasp

The female tarantula hawk wasp (above) locates a tarantula in its underground burrow. The crafty wasp then lures the spider outside by tugging on the silk lines the spider has woven to catch its prey. The battle that follows is brief, as the wasp swiftly stings and paralyzes the tarantula. She drags the huge spider to a specially constructed burrow, where she lays a single egg on its abdomen. After covering the burrow with soil, she leaves. When the egg hatches, the wasp larva will have plenty of food. Most species of tarantula hawk wasp are found in tropical forests, but they also live in the deserts of North America.

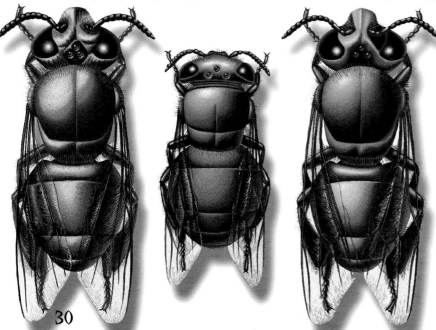

# Orchid Bee

These brightly colored tropical bees (left) have very long tongues with which they can sip the nectar from long-necked flowers such as orchids. The nectar gives the bees energy — they are not only speedy fliers but they can travel great distances, too.

30

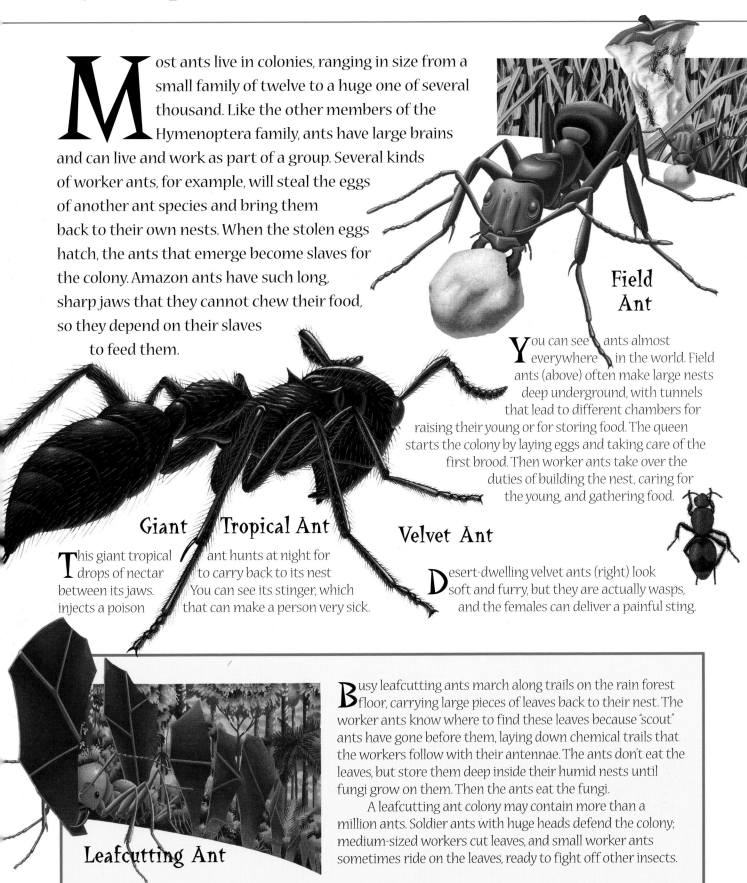

**M**ost ants live in colonies, ranging in size from a small family of twelve to a huge one of several thousand. Like the other members of the Hymenoptera family, ants have large brains and can live and work as part of a group. Several kinds of worker ants, for example, will steal the eggs of another ant species and bring them back to their own nests. When the stolen eggs hatch, the ants that emerge become slaves for the colony. Amazon ants have such long, sharp jaws that they cannot chew their food, so they depend on their slaves to feed them.

## Field Ant

**Y**ou can see ants almost everywhere in the world. Field ants (above) often make large nests deep underground, with tunnels that lead to different chambers for raising their young or for storing food. The queen starts the colony by laying eggs and taking care of the first brood. Then worker ants take over the duties of building the nest, caring for the young, and gathering food.

## Giant Tropical Ant

**T**his giant tropical ant hunts at night for drops of nectar to carry back to its nest between its jaws. You can see its stinger, which injects a poison that can make a person very sick.

## Velvet Ant

**D**esert-dwelling velvet ants (right) look soft and furry, but they are actually wasps, and the females can deliver a painful sting.

## Leafcutting Ant

**B**usy leafcutting ants march along trails on the rain forest floor, carrying large pieces of leaves back to their nest. The worker ants know where to find these leaves because "scout" ants have gone before them, laying down chemical trails that the workers follow with their antennae. The ants don't eat the leaves, but store them deep inside their humid nests until fungi grow on them. Then the ants eat the fungi.

A leafcutting ant colony may contain more than a million ants. Soldier ants with huge heads defend the colony; medium-sized workers cut leaves, and small worker ants sometimes ride on the leaves, ready to fight off other insects.

# Index

# Recommended Reading

*(all age appropriate)*

*The Fascinating World of Beetles* by Maria Angels Julivert, illustrations by Marcel Socias Studios. (Barron's Educational Series, Inc., 1995) All about different kinds of beetles and their interesting behaviors.

*The Big Bug Book* by Margery Facklam, illustrations in actual size by Paul Facklam. (Little, Brown and Company, 1994) A close look at thirteen of the world's largest insects.

*Butterfly and Moth* (Eyewitness Books) by Paul Whalley. (Alfred A. Knopf, New York and Dorling Kindersley, U.K., 1988) Full of stunning photographs of caterpillars, butterflies, and moths found throughout the world.

*Bugs: A closer look at the world's tiny creatures* by Jinny Johnson. (A Reader's Digest Kids Book, 1995) Giant illustrations and informative text bring the extraordinary world of insects to life.

*Insects & Spiders* (The Nature Company Discoveries Library) Consulting editor: George Else & specialist staff, Department of Entomology, The Natural History Museum, London, text by David Burnie. (Time-Life Books, 1997) A detailed illustrated reference book about insects and spiders.

*Insects* (My First Pocket Guide series) by Daniel J. Bickel. (National Geographic Society, 1996) A first field guide to North American insects, complete with maps, illustrations, and photographs.

# Acknowledgments

With many thanks to Dr. Doug Currie and John Swann of the Centre for Biodiversity and Conservation Biology at the Royal Ontario Museum and to Dr. Tim Myles, Faculty of Forestry, University of Toronto, for their expertise and patience; to editors Ian Coutts and Mireille Majoor, who together conceived of the book; to Julian Mulock for his stunning illustrations as well as for being such a pleasure to work with; to Gord Sibley for his outstanding design; to Mireille Majoor and Hugh Brewster for working their magic with the text; to Susan Aihoshi for her generous editorial assistance; to Lloyd Davis for his meticulous copy editing; and to Susan Barrable and Sandra Hall for their production expertise.

*Nan Froman*

First published in 2001 by
Little, Brown and Company
3 Center Plaza
Boston, Massachusetts 02108
U.S.A.

1 3 5 7 9 10 8 6 4 2

Library of Congress Cataloging-in-Publication Data is on file.

ISBN: 0-316-29692-9

*Book Design:*
Gordon Sibley Design Inc.

*Editorial Director:*
Hugh Brewster

*Project Editors:*
Ian Coutts and Mireille Majoor

*Editorial Assistance:*
Susan Aihoshi

*Production Director:*
Susan Barrable

*Production Coordinator:*
Sandra Hall

*Color Separation:*
Colour Technologies

*Printing and Binding:*
EuroGrafica S.p.A., Vicenza

WHAT'S THAT BUG?
was produced by
Madison Press Books,
which is under the direction of
Albert E. Cummings

**Produced by
Madison Press Books
40 Madison Avenue
Toronto, Ontario
Canada M5R 2S1**

*Printed and bound in Italy*